To Emerson and Margie

RINGY DINGY DOUGHNUT-MAKING THINGY©

A Thank-You Song for Christy Ottaviano:
(to be sung to a tune by KC and the Sunshine Band)
Christy, Christy, we work together
Otie, Otie, me and you
You're smart and nice, and give good advice
And I like your hairdo!
Oh, I write a little book, you take a little look,
You make it right, You make it right!
Oh, I write a little book, you take a little look,
You make it right, you make it right!

Henry Holt and Company, *Publishers since 1866*
Henry Holt® is a registered trademark of Macmillan Publishing Group, LLC
120 Broadway, New York, NY 10271 • mackids.com

Copyright © 2020 by Laurie Keller
All rights reserved
Library of Congress Cataloging-in-Publication Data is available.
ISBN 978-1-250-10724-4

Our books may be purchased in bulk for promotional, educational, or business use.
Please contact your local bookseller or the Macmillan Corporate and
Premium Sales Department at (800) 221-7945 ext. 5442
or by email at MacmillanSpecialMarkets@macmillan.com.

First edition, 2020
The illustrations were created with markers, colored pencils, pen and ink,
acrylic paint, collage, and digital drawing.
Printed in China by Toppan Leefung Printing Ltd., Dongguan City, Guangdong Province

1 3 5 7 9 10 8 6 4 2

Hi, Plain!

Good morning, Glazed!

Hey, Long John!

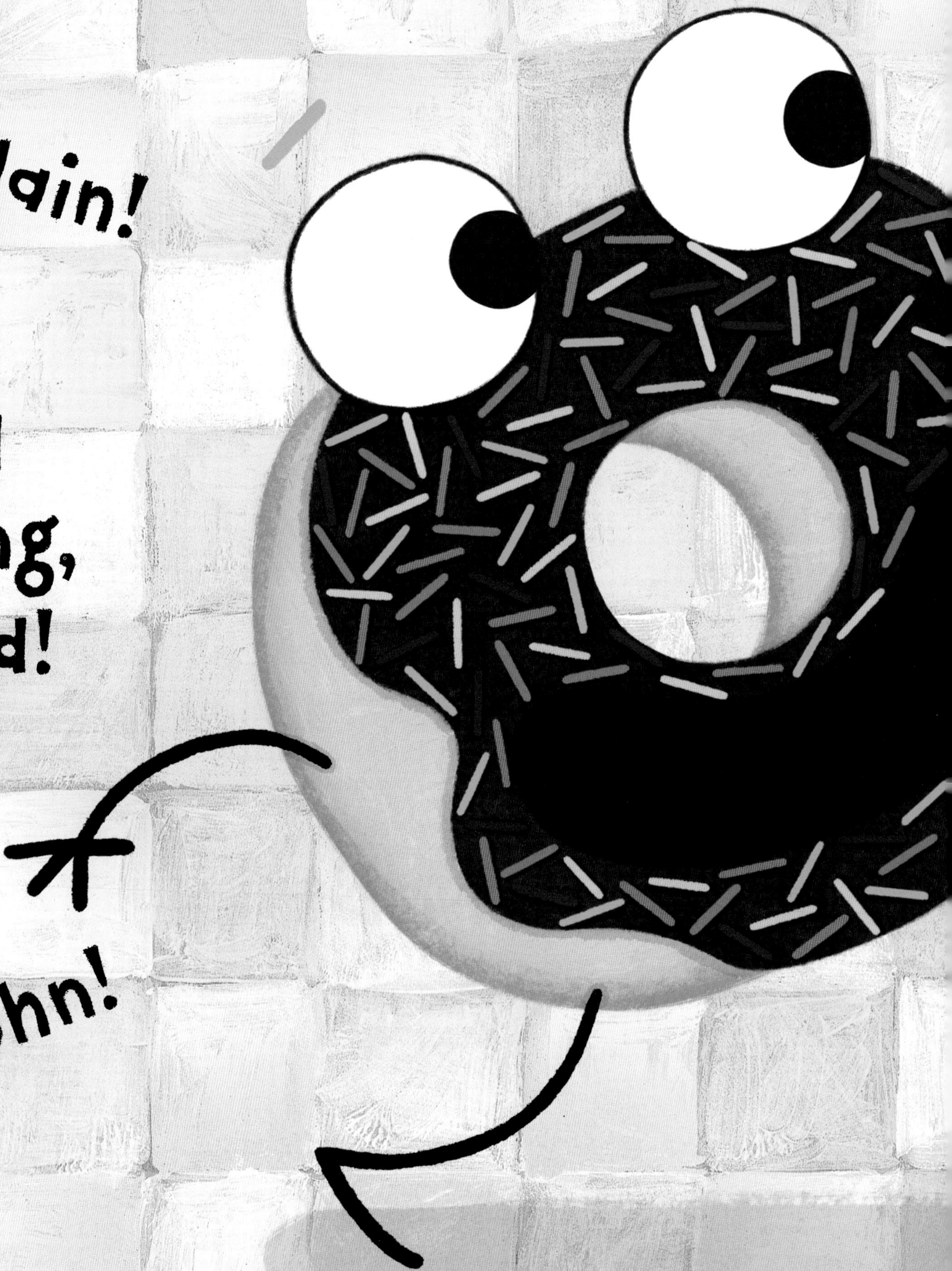

Howdy,
Doughnut Holes!

Pleased to meet
you, Powdered!

Top of the
morning, Jelly!

WOO-HOO!
I know
everyone in
the bakery!

Wait—you
missed one,
Arnie.

I did?
Where?

Right
out
there.

You're . . .
the biggest doughnut . . .
I've ever seen!

You're
bigger
than
all
of
us
put
together!

Mr. Baker Man must have used a whole batch of dough to make YOU!

50 LB

SUGAR

FLOUR

So, what kind of giant doughnut ARE you anyway?

WHAT?! You don't know what kind?

How will you know which doughnut tray to sit on?

Don't worry.
I'll help you
figure it out.

Well, you're not ROUND like I am.

And you're tall, like a Long John.

THAT'S IT!

You're a GIANT LONG JOHN!

Average Long John

Giant Long John

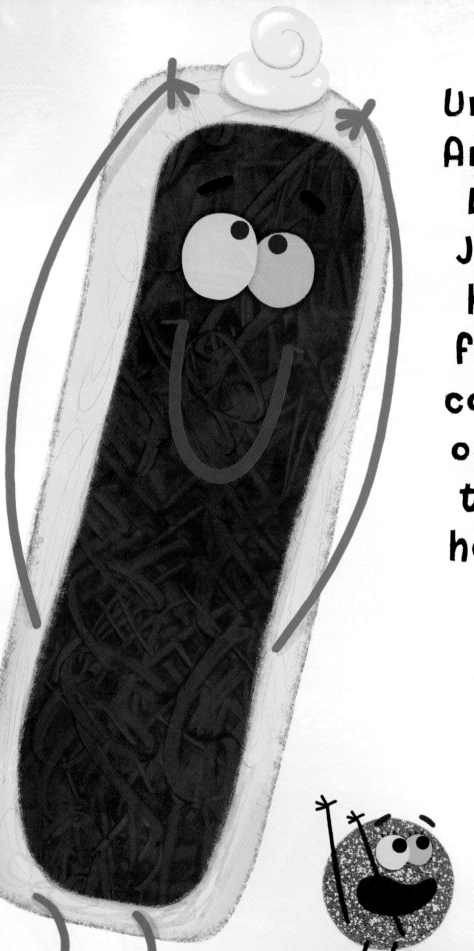

Ummm, Arnie— Long Johns have filling coming out of their heads.

Oh!

Nope.
Not a
Long John.

I can see you
don't have
a hole in
the middle.

But don't worry! I know LOTS of perfectly happy doughnuts with no holes in the middle!

You don't have any frosting or sprinkles.

WHY NOT?

Sprinkles are the **BEST!**

I bet it would take a **MILLION** sprinkles to cover **YOU!**

You'd look good with frosting-sprinkle glasses.

Or a frosting-sprinkle hairdo.

Oh, I know . . . a frosting-sprinkle mustache!

All right, that's enough sprinkle talk for now. It's time to see what kind of giant doughnut you are.

THIS IS SO EXCITING!

Let's see . . .

1. You're not round.

2. You don't have filling coming out of your head.

3. You don't have a hole in the middle.

4. You don't have frosting or sprinkles.

Hmmm, this is harder than I thought.

It's almost like you're not even a doughnut!

Okay, something sticky is going on here. I'm starting to think you're *NOT* a giant doughnut.

Wait—
I know what you are.

You're
a . . .

You're a...

And Mr. Baker Man made you with this **GIANT COOKIE CUTTER,** which looks just like you!

Oh, Giant Cookie . . .
I can't believe I
thought you were
a giant doughnut.

But I still think you'd look good with a frosting-sprinkle mustache!